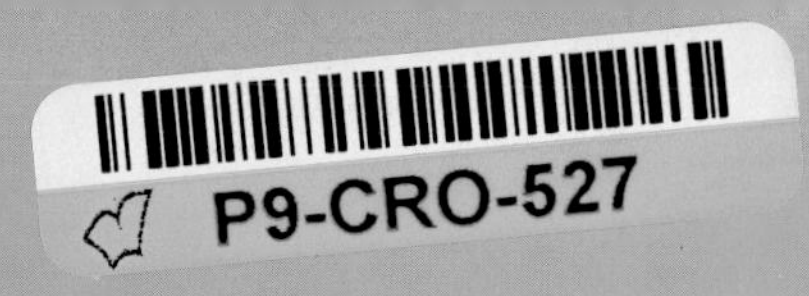

To:

From:

THE BROTHER BOOK

TODD PARR

Megan Tingley Books
LITTLE, BROWN AND COMPANY
NEW YORK BOSTON

To Dominic, Spencer, Gibson, and Jamie

Also by Todd Parr

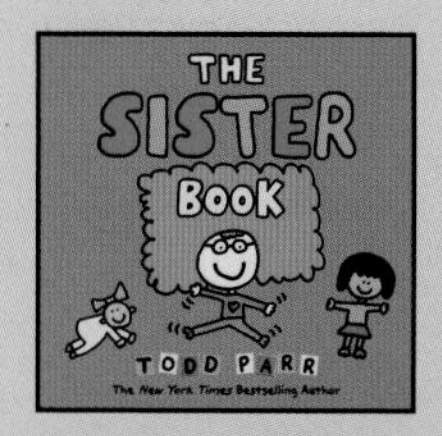

A complete list of Todd's books and more information can be found at toddparr.com.

About This Book

The art for this book was created on a drawing tablet using an iMac, starting with bold black lines and dropping in color with Adobe Photoshop. This book was edited by Megan Tingley and Allison Moore and designed by Nicole Brown. The production was supervised by Erika Schwartz, and the production editor was Marisa Finkelstein. The text was set in Todd Parr's signature font.

 • Little, Brown and Company Hachette Book Group • 1290 Avenue of the Americas, New York, NY 10104 • Visit us at LBYR.com • First Edition: March 2018 • Little, Brown and Company is a division of Hachette Book Group, Inc. The Little, Brown name and logo are trademarks of Hachette Book Group, Inc. • The publisher is not responsible for websites (or their content) that are not owned by the publisher. • Library of Congress Cataloging-in-Publication Data • Names: Parr, Todd, author. • Title: The brother book / Todd Parr. • Description: First edition. | New York ; Boston : Little, Brown and Company, 2018. | "Megan Tingley Books." | Summary: Presents a variety of brothers, some quiet and some wild, some who study bugs and some who eat them, some who look like you and some who do not. • Identifiers: LCCN 2017020290 | ISBN 9780316265171 (hardcover) | ISBN 9780316265164 (ebook) | ISBN 9780316265157 (library edition ebook) • Subjects: | CYAC: Brothers—Fiction. • Classification: LCC PZ7.P2447 Bro 2018 | DDC [E]—dc23 • LC record available at https://lccn.loc.gov/2017020290 • ISBNs: 978-0-316-26517-1 (hardcover), 978-0-316-26516-4 (ebook) • PRINTED IN CHINA • APS • 10 9 8 7 6 5 4 3 2 1

There are all kinds of brothers.

Some brothers are big.

Some brothers are little.

Some brothers are quiet.

Some brothers are a little wild.

Some brothers like to hang out with you.

Some brothers like to spend time alone.

Some brothers yell when they are upset.

Some brothers cry.

Some brothers like to play house.

Some brothers like to play trucks.

Some brothers like to play sports.

Some brothers like to dance.

Some brothers study bugs.

Some brothers eat bugs.

Some brothers look like you.

Some brothers look like themselves.

Some brothers live nearby.

Some brothers live far away.

All brothers are a special

part of your family!

Brothers are very special.

Sometimes they hug you, and sometimes they bug you. Be sure to tell them how much you love them.

The End. ♥ Love, Todd